EATER

S EVER SEEN!

Wash
ts

¢

ailor

BUTLER TREMONT STORES

A New Store for LITTLE CHILDREN

Children's 49¢
Rompers

At **29¢**

ALL SIZES

Children's 69¢
French Dresses

At **49¢**

ALL SIZES

NOTICE NEW LOCATIONS,
NEW MERCHANDISE

NOW ON THIRD FLOOR

THE GRANT CAR

$495
COMPLETE
F.O.B. FACT

"THE CLASS

First Edition
1 3 5 7 9 10 8 6 4 2
Printed in Singapore
Library of Congress Cataloging-in-Publication Data on file.
ISBN 978-1-4231-1390-4
Designed by Elizabeth H. Clark
Reinforced binding
Visit www.hyperionbooksforchildren.com

PENNIES FOR
ELEPHANTS
by
LITA JUDGE

Disney · HYPERION BOOKS
NEW YORK

"Henry, look. Elephants!"
I'd only seen elephants once in real life, when Grams
took Henry and me to the circus.
They were my favorite. Henry's too.

The Boston Post

MONDAY MARCH 9 1914

THREE TRAINED PACHYDERMS FOR SALE!

Famous performing elephants salute children of Boston. Their names are Mollie, Tony, and Waddy.

Mr. and Mrs. William Orford, noted animal trainers, are retiring from show business. City can't afford to buy the elephants for the zoo, but Orfords agree to give the children of Boston two months to collect $6,000. Just imagine, kids—you could ride elephants at the zoo someday!

"Come on, Dorothy." Henry grabbed my hand and raced toward home.
When Henry got an idea in his head, it was like fuel to a Studebaker.

"Get your piggy bank," he said, breaking open his own. Pennies and nickels spilled onto the floor.

Grams took us to the *Boston Post*, where they were collecting money for the elephant fund. Henry and I plopped down one dollar and fourteen cents, our entire life savings combined.

That night it snowed.

LONDON ZOO OFFERS $6,000 ON THE SPOT FOR TRAINED ELEPHANTS!

Must earn the money now. No time to waste!

$.03 from three-year-old Anna

$.25 from Anthony—his movie money. "I'd much rather it go to the elephant fund."

$.05 from Jimmy— the nickel the tooth fairy left for his front tooth.

$.18 from Frances—"To buy part of Tony's ear so he will hear me when I visit him at the zoo."

$1.14 Henry and Dorothy contribute life savings.

I woke Henry early the next morning. Usually I hated shoveling snow, but not that day. We knocked at all the neighbors' doors and offered to clear their stoops for a nickel.

News about the elephants must have spread throughout the city, because there was a whole army of us kids shoveling snow. "All proceeds go to the elephants!" we cheered.

WILDERMUTH

Every morning we searched the paper for news about the elephants, and we always discovered something. "We can visit them at the stables!" Henry said.

WEST COAST CIRCUS OFFERS TO BUY ELEPHANTS!

Kids of Boston raise only $1,230 so far.

Henry and I went to see Mollie, Waddy, and Tony right away.
"We can't let the circus take them," I told Henry. "We have to do more."

Henry and I decided to host the biggest costume party anyone had ever seen, and charge admission. Everyone was invited to dress like their favorite zoo animal. I trained Beatrix to do tricks.

At least I tried to.

BROTHER AND SISTER,
HENRY AND DOROTHY, EARNED $.87
HOSTING ELEPHANT FUND PARTY!

$.05—Emily irons handkerchiefs for her mother.

$.15—Ethel runs errands for her auntie.

$.67—Walter bakes cupcakes and cookies to sell at his father's shop.

$.48—Amanda sells homemade fudge door to door.

Then the *Boston Post* invited Henry and me to a tea party with Mollie, Waddy, and Tony! Mollie and Waddy did tricks.

Baby Tony reached into my pocket for the sugar cubes I had hidden as a treat. Grams laughed so hard she spilled her tea.

"Three thousand dollars. Halfway point!" shouted the paper boy. "Still three thousand to go!"

Soon, so many of us kids refused to spend our money, the theaters started hosting moving picture shows with ticket sales going to the elephant fund.

ELEPHANT
CLIMBS TO

Army of children
raise funds for M
$.07—Tommy we
$.78—Joe and Sa
$.63—Beth and
$.15—Wendy bri
Scott holds
wor

$700 TO GO—ONLY TWO WEEKS LEFT TO RAISE THE MONEY!

Kids from all over New England now join the effort as news of the elephants spreads. They send in money from Maine, New Hampshire, and Vermont!

$.14 from Roger for washing 14 windows.

$1.02—Ronny hosts pirate costume party.

$.22—Little Francis sold his toy elephant to earn money for the real elephants.

$1.40—Charles Wright plays his violin and Virginia Smith sings in concert to packed audience.

$.82—Steven puts on magic show.

$1.19—Kids earn money washing neighborhood pets.

BABY TONY CONTRIBUTES SHINY DIME TO HIS OWN FUND!

It's true! Tony, that clever little elephant, found a dime while playing in the stable yard. The curious rascal is constantly searching for treats, and today he discovered a dime in the gutter. Not liking the taste of it, he tossed it on the table where a tea party was being held for the elephant fund. Good job, Tony!

CHILDREN OF NEW ENGLAND HAVE DONE IT!
MORE THAN $6,000 RAISED FOR ELEPHANT FUND!

Come to Fenway Park next Saturday for the great event! Huge crowd expected. More than 50,000 children sent money! Governor will present elephants to Mayor Curley on behalf of the children.

"The elephants are going to parade through Boston. Marching bands and drum corps—the works!" Henry read.

We raced to the *Boston Post* and signed up to be in the marching band.

I told baby Tony about the parade, and the governor coming, and how many people would be there. I told him every detail, over and over—so he wouldn't be nervous.

At last, the day arrived! Every seat was filled, and crowds spilled out onto the field as we marched into Fenway Park.

Mollie, Waddy, and Tony trumpeted so loudly, they sounded like their own brass band.

Then the governor presented the elephants to the mayor. He tried to be very serious, but when Tony searched his pockets for a treat, everyone laughed.

We kids had done it! All of Boston cheered.

Mollie, Waddy, and Tony were home to stay.